FROM THE LAND OF THE WHITE BIRCH

Written by Shirley Neitzel
Pictures by Daniel Powers

River Road Publications, Inc.
Spring Lake, Michigan

Dedication
For my husband, Eric
— SN

To my illustration critique group members:
Lori, Jill; Elizabeth, Teresa, Amy, Lynn;
Margy, Caroline, Rex; and to Silke
— DP

First U.S. edition 1997

Library of Congress Cataloging-in-Publication Data
From the Land of the White Birch/Shirley Neitzel, Daniel Powers
ISBN 0-938682-44-X; Paperback ISBN 0-938682-56-3

E99. C6N38 1997   97-9603
398.2 '089973 – dc21   CIP AC

River Road Publications, Inc.
Spring Lake, MI

FROM THE
LAND
OF THE
WHITE BIRCH

The Sun Snarer

LONG AGO, when the mouse wore a beautiful white fur coat and was a very large animal, bigger than even a bear, a boy and his sister lived by themselves in the forest. Their parents and all the other people of their village had died, so the girl looked after her brother who was very small.

One day Sister gave Little Brother a bow and arrows that were just his size. "Practice with these," she said.

"Thank you, Sister. One day I will be a great hunter and will kill a mouse. Its white fur will make a fine robe to sleep on."

Sister smiled fondly at Little Brother. "Yes, but practice on smaller animals first," she said as she went to gather wood for their fire.

All day Little Brother worked with the bow. Before long he was able to hit the trunk of the tree. Pleased with himself, he pointed his bow toward a snowbird that had come to feed in the white birch. His aim was true, and when Sister came home he boasted.

"Look. I have shot a snowbird. I would like you to skin it for me. Then each day I will hunt for more. When I have enough, I want you to make a coat for me."

"All right," Sister said, "I'll make you a coat. But when you shoot a mouse you must give me its beautiful white fur for a robe."

Each day Little Brother went out with his bow. When he came home in the evening Sister skinned the snowbirds he brought her and stretched their feathered hides.

When Sister had ten bird skins, she made them into a beautiful feather coat. It fit Little Brother perfectly. He was proud of it.

"Sister, I want to show my wonderful coat to other people. Where do they live?"

"Our mother and father once spoke of a village far away toward the rising sun. But it is a long way. Do not go, Little Brother. It is too far for one as small as you."

Little Brother did not think he was too small for such a journey, and he was eager to meet other people. He waited until Sister went to gather food. Then he set out to find the village.

Little Brother walked for a very long time—up hill and down, through forest and across streams. Finally, when the moon was high in the sky, he came to a meadow. He gathered grass and ferns into a pile to make a bed. He took off his fine feather coat. Then he lay down to rest, pulling it over him like a blanket.

While he was sleeping the moon set. The sun poked its head over the hill-top. Still Little Brother slept. As it rose higher, the sun became very hot and scorched the feathers of Little Brother's coat. The skins shrank and tore where they were stitched together.

The sun was high in the sky when Little Brother awoke. He was angry to see his coat ruined. He shook his fist at the sun. "You will be sorry for this trick!"

Carrying his coat, which was now much too small and ugly to wear, he returned home to Sister.

"Look what the sun did to my beautiful coat," he said. "Give me some thread. I am going to make a snare to catch the sun."

"No, Little Brother, such a trick would be very dangerous." Still, when she saw he was determined, she offered him a cord she had twisted from grass.

"That is not strong enough," he said.

Looking in her bag again, Sister pulled out a piece of sinew. "I used this to sew the coat," she said.

"No," he pouted. "That will not do. You saw how the sun split the seams. Find something else."

Sister frowned. She had no other thread. Then she had an idea. She cut some of her hair and offered it to Little Brother.

Little Brother's face brightened as he gently pulled the silky black strands through his fingers. "Yes, I will use this," he said. "If the beautiful hair of Sister is not strong enough to hold the sun, nothing is!"

Little Brother spent many hours braiding the hair until he had a strong cord. Then he tied it into a noose. Now, he thought, I am ready to snare the sun.

The next day Little Brother set out toward the east. He journeyed up hill and down, through the forest, and across streams. Finally he found the place where the sun had burned his coat.

Carefully Little Brother laid his snare at the place the sun would travel in the morning. Then he went to a safe place where he could hide and watch his trap.

The night seemed very long to Little Brother, but at last the moon set in the west. Slowly the sun poked its head up over the hill. Little Brother held his breath as it moved toward his snare. The snare caught the sun fast and struggle though it might, it could not get away.

"A-ha," Little Brother called. "I have caught you. As punishment for spoiling my beautiful feather coat, you shall stay right there!" Then, happy that his plan had worked, he set out for home.

With the sun stuck on the hilltop, the land remained in twilight throughout the day. The forest animals were afraid and called a meeting. Owl reported that while he was hunting he had found the sun tied to the earth.

"Chipmunk," said Owl, "you are a cheeky fellow. You could go and cut the cord that holds the sun."

"N-n-no," chattered Chipmunk. "The sun is so hot there would be nothing left of me if I went near. Beaver, you are much larger than I, and your teeth are strong enough to cut down trees. You should go and cut the cord."

"I will try," said Beaver. So, holding his tail over his back as a shield, he made his way up the hill. He had only gone a short way when the hair on his tail caught fire from the sun's rays. Beaver wheeled around and plunged into the pond. From the water he called out. "Bear, you are larger and stronger than I, you must try to free the sun."

So Bear lumbered up the hill. As he got closer his fur began to smoke, but he walked on steadily. Surely, he thought, he could snap the cord with one bite of his powerful jaws. He shut his eyes tight to block the sun's brightness and opened his mouth wide. Then, thrusting his head forward to bite the cord, his nose bumped the sun. Immediately it was burned as black as a raven's wing. Howling with pain, Bear ran back down the hill.

"Mouse," he cried. "You are larger and stronger than I. You must try to free the sun."

"Yes," Mouse answered, for at that time she was larger and stronger. "It is my duty. I will try."

So Mouse went to the top of the hill and quickly began gnawing the snare. Although she felt the heat melting her body, Mouse kept on chewing. Her fur began to smoke and her back burned to ashes, but still she gnawed. Finally, when there was hardly anything left of her, the last hair thread snapped.

The struggling sun leaped to the sky. Happy to be free, it shone brighter and warmer than ever as it continued its journey to the west.

The animals rejoiced to have the sunlight once again. Bear with his shiny black nose and sooty fur danced with Beaver with his hairless tail. But poor brave Mouse hid in the shadows. Her beautiful white fur was now the color of ashes. Although once the largest of animals, she was now the smallest.

So, to this day, do not expect to see a mouse until twilight. She is still fearful the sun may burn her completely away. As for Little Brother who caused all the trouble, he became a very skillful hunter. But without a white mouse robe for his sister, he could not convince her to make him a new feather coat.

Ojeeg's Search for Summer

IN THE DAYS OF EVERLASTING WINTER Ojeeg lived with his wife and young son on the shores of a great lake. Now Ojeeg was an expert hunter. His totem was a fisher, a member of the weasel family— all skilled hunters. But in the biting wind and deep snow that always lay on the ground, even Ojeeg had a hard time finding food for his family.

Ojeeg's son wished to be a hunter, also. Ojeeg made a bow for him of hickory wood and arrows from the straightest ash tree. Each day the boy practiced until his fingers were too numb with cold to draw his bowstring tight.

One day as the boy drew the sinew taut across his bow, the squirrel he was stalking spoke to him. "Do not shoot me, Son of Ojeeg."

The boy was surprised and lowered his bow. "You know me and my father!"

"Yes, you are the son of the mighty Ojeeg. But a hunter must be wise as well as skillful."

"But you know I must bring my family food so they will not die of hunger."

"One squirrel will not satisfy your hunger. It is Ojeeg who can spare us all the pain and hunger caused by this everlasting winter. He has the power, and he will use it if it is you who asks."

"That would be a very great thing," said Ojeeg's son.

"Then listen carefully. You must go home without game. Throw down your bow and arrows. Weep. When your mother offers you food, do not eat it. Refuse to be comforted. When your father sees you so upset he will ask what he can do. Tell him the Sky People keep the birds of summer locked in cages. If he will set them free, we will have warm weather here below. Food will be plentiful for you and for us, your animal brothers."

Ojeeg's son thought for a long time. Then he picked up his empty game bag and nodded to the squirrel to show he agreed with the plan.

When he reached home he threw his bow and arrows on the ground and wept bitterly.

"My son, why do you weep?" his mother asked. "Come warm yourself by the fire and eat. I have saved this fine bit of venison for you."

The boy pushed away the food and cried even harder.

Soon Ojeeg came from the forest. "Tell me, Son, what is it that troubles you? I would do anything in my power to take away your pain and sadness."

"Oh Father, you have the power to end this everlasting winter." The boy sobbed and repeated everything that the squirrel had told him.

When he finished Ojeeg said, "It is a hard thing to do, my Son, but I will try."

Ojeeg called a meeting of the tribe. "A manitou in the form of a squirrel has spoken to my son. He told him of a way to soften the wind and melt the snow of everlasting winter. I am going to the Land Beyond the Sky to release the birds of summer. It will be dangerous. Who is brave enough to go with me?"

"I will go," said one. "And I," said another. "And I," said a third.

Ojeeg nodded to his friends. "Prepare for a long journey and say good-bye to your families. You may not see them again."

Then Ojeeg filled a pouch with pemmican his wife had made of dried berries and nuts. He filled another with dried venison. In the morning the four set

out. Each carried enough food to last until the old woman in the moon would waste away and once again grow fat.

For days the men trudged in the snow and cold. On the twentieth day they rested on the top of a high mountain. The sky seemed very close. Ojeeg took out his pipe, lit it, and offered smoke to the four winds, the sky, and the earth. Then he spoke in a loud voice. "Oh Great Spirit, help me in my mission to bring summer to earth for my son and for my people, that their suffering and starvation may be at an end."

Looking at his companions, Ojeeg saw the Great Spirit had allowed them to take the forms of their animal totems. He himself had the sleek fur and strong body of the fisher. One man became an otter. Another was now a wolverine. The third was a badger.

"Let us leap to the sky," Ojeeg said. "Who will be first?"

"I will," said Badger. He jumped with all his might. His head struck the sky with a mighty blow. Stunned, he fell back to earth where he lay very still.

Next, Otter bounded upward. When he struck the sky he flipped upside down, fell, and slid down the mountainside. He scrambled back to the top just as Badger was getting to his feet.

Then Wolverine tried. He bunched his muscles for a mighty leap and struck the sky with his powerful shoulders.

"Again!" shouted Ojeeg. "You have cracked the sky."

Again and again Wolverine jumped. Each time he bumped the sky the crack became larger. At last there was a hole big enough to crawl through.

Climbing on Wolverine's shoulders Ojeeg crawled through the hole. Then he reached down and helped the others until they were all in the Land Beyond the Sky.

Ojeeg looked about with wonder. The warm air ruffled his fur. Flowers of all the colors of the rainbow filled his nostrils with their sweet smell. The animals rolled in the soft, damp grass.

Otter discovered a path that led to a stream. Unlike the ice-covered streams they knew on earth, this one sparkled in the sunshine as it bubbled and gurgled its way over stones. Tree branches, heavy with fruit, bent low over the water.

Rounding a bend of the stream Ojeeg and the animals came to a group of wigwams. "This must be the village of the Sky People," Ojeeg said. "Walk softly."

The animals looked this way and that. "I do not see anyone," said Wolverine. "Perhaps the Sky People are away."

Ojeeg crept to the largest wigwam. Quietly he lifted the buckskin that covered the doorway, and the animals slipped inside. In the dim light from the smoke hole, Ojeeg saw the wigwam was lined with many birch bark boxes tied with rawhide. From them came the warbling and twitters of many soft voices.

"These must be the birds of summer," Ojeeg whispered as he untied the rawhide knots. When he lifted the lid thrushes and warblers flew out. "Hurry," he urged them. "Fly through the hole in the sky and down to earth."

The second box had finches and sparrows. Another held jays and wrens. Ojeeg hurried around the wigwam freeing the birds. Swallows, woodpeckers, and bluebirds rose like a colorful cloud and flew toward the hole in the sky.

Otter peered down from the edge of the hole. He felt the rush of warm air and watched the birds glide to earth. "The snow is melting," he called. "The trees are turning green."

Ojeeg heard Otter shouting. Then a terrible cry filled the air. "Stop thieves!" The Sky People came running. "You are stealing our warm weather."

Ojeeg struggled to open the last box before the Sky People heard him, too. "Hurry to earth," he whispered to the swarm of hummingbirds that escaped as the rawhide snapped.

Then Ojeeg called to Wolverine and Badger, "Run. Follow Otter back to earth before the Sky People capture you."

To give his friends a chance to escape, he called to the Sky People. "I have taken your warmth and your birds." Then he ran in the opposite direction of the hole.

The Sky People chased him, shaking their fists and shouting.

Ojeeg scrambled to the top of the tallest pine and mocked the Sky People. "Your arrows are useless against me. I am Ojeeg, the mighty hunter."

The Sky People showered him with arrows. They did not know the only place Ojeeg could be harmed was a small spot on his tail. As the last of the birds escaped through the hole in the sky, an arrow found the mark.

Ojeeg knew he was dying. "My son," he cried. "I have kept my promise. Although it has cost me my life, I am happy knowing the earth will no longer suffer from everlasting winter." Then his eyes closed.

Because he had kept his promise, the Great Spirit looked kindly on Ojeeg. He placed him in the northern sky where he was able to look down and see his son grow to become a fine hunter. Every year he sees the birds build their nests in the forest, and when the warm winds melt the snow, he is happy.

So on a warm night look to the stars. Find the fisher with the arrow in his tail, and remember brave Ojeeg who traveled to the Land Beyond the Sky so that the earth might have summer.

In the northern sky are a group of stars the Ojibwa call Ojeeg Annung, the fisher stars. You may know them as the Big Dipper.

Wassamowin
and the Thunderbirds

ONCE LONG AGO, Wassamowin was returning from a hunt with two fine beaver he had speared. It was early springtime, and the soft muddy earth made travel slow. Ice still covered the lakes, but it was soft and slushy, so Wassamowin could not walk over them.

The sun was far along in its westward journey. Wassamowin's hunt had taken him far from home, and he still had a long way to go. His wife and children would be worried, but Wassamowin was not. His spear was fast as lightning; it would protect him. He was not afraid of the coming night.

There was only one thing Wassamowin feared—Animiki, the thunderbird who lived in the mountains. This huge bird sometimes appeared at night and frightened people with the roar of its wings and the fire that shot from its eyes. It was said that if the bird appeared before the sun had set, something very bad would happen to anyone who saw it.

As the sun slipped toward the horizon, a strange shadow covered Wassamowin's path. The brave hunter looked up and recognized Animiki. His heart pounded, and he crouched low along the path like a field mouse hiding from a hawk. Wassamowin hoped the thunderbird would pass without seeing him, but that was not to be. He felt the rush of wind as the bird swooped down and grabbed him.

The roar of the bird's wings blocked out Wassamowin's cries as they flew westward toward the mountains. After what seemed like an endless flight Animiki circled a rocky peak, and Wassamowin looked down into a large nest among the rocks. In it were two enormous young thunderbirds. The nestlings stretched their necks and flapped their wings with excitement at their parent's return. As they jostled each other, Wassawomin judged the young birds' wingspan to be nearly the same as his outstretched arms.

Hovering near the nest, Animiki swung Wassamowin around and around. For a time it seemed the hunter would be smashed against the boulders. But he held his spear tightly, turning it quickly one way and then another. As he did so, the spear took the force of the blows, and he was able to keep his body from striking the rocks. At last the thunderbird tired of the game, dropped him into the nest with the two young birds, and flew off.

Squawking noisily, the nestlings eagerly attacked this strange creature that had been brought to them. They snapped at him with long hooked beaks. Their sharp claws tore his buckskin shirt and leggings. With each blink, fire flashed from their eyes and scorched Wassamowin's hands and face. Although he defended himself bravely, Wassawomin feared he would soon be overpowered.

Suddenly Wassamowin remembered the beavers he had speared to provide food for his family. He took one from his shoulder strap and threw it toward the young birds. Both of them snapped for it. While the two nestlings fought over the first beaver, Wassamowin tied a strong cord to the second one. Holding an end of the cord, Wassamowin waited until one of the birds glanced his way. Then he tossed the beaver upward. The young thunderbird grabbed and swallowed it in mid-air.

Holding fast to the cord, Wassamowin jumped onto the young bird's back. Using the cord as reins, Wassamowin kicked the nestling and urged it to fly. Never having flown, the awkward bird began stumbling down the mountainside. As it bounded from rock to rock, its feathers flashed with fire.

Suddenly the bird stumbled and with its rider fell off the edge of the cliff. Just when Wassamowin thought he and the young bird would plunge to their death, he felt the thunderbird's wings spread. Instantly they caught the wind. As if it had always flown, the young bird soared over the countryside with Wassamowin on its back.

After they were far from the thunderbird's mountain home, Wassamowin pulled on the cord until he forced the thunderbird to the ground. Then he released the bird and shouted, "Go, and be thankful that I, Wassamowin, am setting you free." With a great roar of wings the young thunderbird flew away.

Wassamowin rested and filled his pipe with tobacco. Pointing it to the four winds, the sky, and the earth, he thanked Kitchi Manitou, the Great Spirit, for his safety. Then he continued his journey home.

Wassamowin's wife and children were very happy to see him. He told them of his adventure and how sorry he was to return without food for them. His wife said it did not matter. She was glad to have him home safely.

For the remainder of the spring and throughout the summer the mountains were wrapped in heavy clouds. The weather was stormy as the thunderbirds moved their home to the taller mountains far to the west where they would be safe from humans.

It has been a long time since anyone has seen the thunderbirds. It is said they now fly above the clouds, much higher than before. So when you hear the roar of their wings or see the fire that flashes from their eyes, don't be afraid. The thunderbirds no longer hunt for people. They are on their way to the ocean to find fish for food.